FRESH FAIRY TALES
VOLUME I

BY DON MILTON

Hi, I'm Don Milton. I spend most of my days in San Tan Village, Gilbert. I hope to meet you soon in person. Feel free to visit whenever you like, during normal business hours of course. We can talk about fairy tales or whatever else you'd like. I'm looking forward to it. I hope you are too! Here's wishing you a fairy tale life!

ISBN: 9781611910049

THIS BOOK IS
DEDICATED TO THOSE
WHO LIVE FAIRY TALE LIVES,
FULL OF TRUTH AND HONOR,
FOR THEY WILL NOT WALK ALONE.

TABLE OF CONTENTS

FRESH FAIRY TALES VOLUME 1 BY DON MILTON

SKETCHES BY NACHO L. GARCIA JR.

POOL OF VANITIES

Once upon a time in a valley deep, over the mountains that divide the great lands, lived a gentle and obedient daughter.

Her mother blessed the house with song while the daughter cooked, cleaned house, and rocked the baby's cradle.

Her father was an oarsman, taking passengers up and down the river for a small fee. Though they were poor, their happiness was unequalled in all the kingdom.

One day when the daughter was going to fetch water from the brook that ran past their stalks of corn, she heard distant voices in the forest.

One was a woman's voice and the other, that of a man. It seemed they were having an argument over which was better; vanity & riches, or happiness.

For those of you who are new to the words of fairy tales, the word vanity means to worship yourself, to think you're better than anyone else.

Now the voice of the woman was for vanity and riches while the voice of the man argued for nothing but happiness. The girl was curious who this could be so she ventured closer and discovered that the voices were coming from a pool of water.

She looked into the pool and saw a reflection of herself wearing the finest of apparel and the crown of a princess though she wore no such clothing.

Then she heard the woman's voice again, this time speaking to her. The woman called her a maiden. Now if you don't know, a maiden is a woman who is old enough to marry but has never been kissed. That was the polite word for any young woman in fairy tale times. Now the voice from the pool called out to the maiden.

"Take a drink young maiden for vanity brings much and the bounty of the king's table beckons you." *Beckon means to call you.* "The clothing and the crown you see in the pool's reflection shall be yours if you but take a drink. Even the wise King Solomon said, happiness is better with riches."

The girl put her hand in the water and stirred it up, scolding the voice that spoke to her,

"Solomon also said, 'Vanity, vanity, all is vanity.' If I want vanity I need look no further than my own mirror for I take no small amount of satisfaction in my own beauty. Even so, my family loves me and forgives me my false pride. Why should I, a maiden, take pride in the beauty which was bestowed on me at birth? No, I shall render due thanks to the creator from which it came. My father reminds me often that a heart full of vanities is empty while a heart full of thanks overflows."

Then the maiden left in a rush for she feared what vain spell the pool might cast upon her.

A few weeks later, as the full moon shown, she could hear the voices once again discussing which was better, vanity and riches, or happiness.

Though she feared the enchantment of the pool she ventured nearer and again saw a reflection of herself, not as she was, but wearing twin gold bracelets with sparkling stones. She almost lifted her arms to gaze upon them but quickly stirred the water.

"Such trifles, bracelets can be." She said. "They gather dough when making bread and their brightness tires the eyes. May I be never so low as to be enchanted by them or so high that I cannot look from a distance with thanks in my heart for those wealthy enough to own them."

Then the girl left in a rush for she feared what spell the pool of vanities might cast upon her.

For weeks the maiden had happily tended to her household chores without giving further thought to the voices. Then one black night there was no moon. She heard them once again.

This time she could make out a man's voice.

"The damsel is obviously immune to your charms or at least is simple enough not to choose for herself but for her family's best interests." *Damsel is a word they use in fairy tales also. It simply means woman.*

To this, the woman's voice from the pool of vanities replied, "Words flow like water but shall you wager that your words are true?"

"What wager do you offer?" The voice of the man replied.

"I wager that the maiden shall not be immune to the charms of vanity if presented by a man whose speech and dress she deems worthy of her love."

"And what have I to gain from this wager?" He said.

"You shall gain your freedom from the spell which cast you, a vain prince, into this pool of vanities. That is, if the girl shuns vanity."

"And if she does not?" He asked.

"You shall lose your soul, for you shall watch as I destroy this young maiden's life. She shall have vanities and pleasures, such as no woman has ever had!"

"I would lose my soul the moment I made such a wager." He replied "May the maiden be kept safe from your treachery! It was your deception that vanity could bring happiness that caused me, a prince, to fall into this pool of vanities and the same trick that landed me here has no power to free but only power to deceive. May the world be kept safe from your vanities!"

The girl was curious at the wise words of the prince so she approached as close as she could get to the pool of vanities. Then suddenly, the waters of the pool began to rise for the prince was weeping enormous tears. *Weep or wept, is the word they like to use in fairy tales for crying.* Now his tears so filled the pool that it began to rise up like a spring.

"Woe!" he said as he wept. "Woe that others shall fall

into the pool of vanities before they have tasted the simple pleasures of a happy home." *Now, woe, is the word that people use in fairy tales when something very bad happens. The prince has a few more woes till he's done so please be patient with him. He's been trapped inside that pool of vanities for many years and he's not feeling very happy right now*. The prince continued to weep and cry out. "Woe that others might drown in this pool before finding out that vanity is empty. Woe that such a destiny as mine would befall the obedient daughter whose family lives so happily in the forest. Woe that anyone else might be trapped inside this pool of vanities as I have been these many years!"

The prince continued weeping till the pool overflowed, becoming a flood upon the land. The maiden was so frightened that she ran home, the waters of the pool lapping at her ankles.

By the time she got home her whole family was huddled in the corner of their hut fearing the worst. By this time, the flood had lifted up their home and cast it down the valley.

Their hut was tossed on the waters all the way to the king's castle and through the gates where it was dashed to pieces inside the king's courtyard.

Then, crawling out from the waters that lapped up from the flood, appeared a man in royal attire. *That's another way of saying fancy clothes.* It was the prince!

The king jumped up from his table shouting thanks till his lungs nearly burst.

"Who has freed my son from the curse of the pool of vanities?" He said.

The prince stood up, then replied,
"This maiden sprawled at our feet has freed me for she shunned vanity and chose happiness and she so moved my heart with love and so filled my soul with happiness at her wise and modest words that my tears burst forth and as you can now see, the curse of the pool of vanities is broken."

"Bring the maiden to my table," the king said, "that I might look upon the one whose wise words freed my son."

The maiden was brought to the king's table where his servants had prepared a place for her. Then the king lifted his cup and proclaimed.

"Let it be ever known in this kingdom that vanity is not befitting a prince or his princess and that my son and his bride shall forevermore dress modestly, eat modestly and spend modestly, and rule with equity."

"And what dowry will you give for my daughter?"
The maiden's father asked.

A dowry is what is given to the father of the bride in fairy tales so that everyone in the kingdom will know that each and every maiden is very precious.

So the king replied to the maiden's father,
"Your dowry shall be to eat from the king's table, you and your family, and to live in my castle but you must continue to work as an oarsman or you must leave the castle, for a man's work keeps him young and I want only blessings for the family of my son's wife."

The father of the maiden quickly agreed and the Prince and his new Princess became husband and wife.

And they lived happily ever after.

For there is no greater dowry, greater in all the world, than for a man to love his work and to have a full plate at the king's table.

Is what the maiden said in the story true? Is it really better to be thankful for our blessings than to want to show off? I think so, don't you? The next fairy tale is called:

The Forest Hermit

A hermit is someone who lives all alone and far from anyone else.

THE FOREST HERMIT

Once upon a time there was a maiden who lived deep in the forest. As she was walking one day, she found a book with wise sayings and so she put it safely in her room and would read it daily. Soon she could recite whole passages from memory and would wonder at their meaning as she read them over and over. She grew wise, not in worldly ways but in a quiet and simple life, loving her family and treating her neighbors with respect. Soon she yearned to know others who might know about the book's wisdom and who could give her more instruction. She hoped on this desire for some time. Her parents and her brothers and sisters joined in her great pleasure at the wisdom found in the book. They also desired to meet others who might know of the book's wisdom.

As the maiden went for one of her daily walks in the forest, she came upon a path, a path that she had not followed before. At the end of the path lay the house of a hermit, a lonely looking man who kept pacing. As he paced back and forth he talked to himself and she believed she heard some passages from the book that she so loved reading. When the man stepped in his house she could not resist but quietly walked up to the window and peered in. Immediately, the man looked up, and saw her, then he shouted.

"Why is it that you stand there peering in at me? You rude and vulgar girl. If you are not a thief, I pray, enter my dwelling and declare yourself a friend. If not, then be gone with you for I have no time for the world and for silly girls."

"I am so sorry sir," the maiden said, "I did not mean to present myself as a thief but I heard your words that sounded so much like the words in a book I have come to love. Please forgive me. And as for entering, I cannot, for I am a maiden and am forbidden the company of men, if my father is not present."

To this the hermit replied,

"Wisely said, young maiden. Now cast aside those beautiful slippers for they do not befit a modest woman such as yourself."

The maiden did not want to cast aside her beloved slippers for they were a gift from her favorite aunt but fearing that her own vanity might cause the old hermit to stumble, and knowing that her aunt would understand, she took off her beloved slippers and cast them into a deep ravine and walked home without shoes.

The next week as she was walking through the forest she heard the hermit talking to himself again and ventured closer to hear what he might say. Again, he was saying something that sounded very much like what she'd read in her book so she came closer that she might listen. This time the hermit shouted even louder.

"You rude and vulgar girl. If you are not a thief, I pray, enter my dwelling and declare yourself a friend. If not, then be gone with you for I have no time for the world and for silly girls."

This time as before, she answered,

"I am so sorry sir. I did not mean to present myself as a thief but I heard your words that sounded so much like the words of a book I have come to love. Please forgive me. And as for entering, I cannot, for I am a maiden and am forbidden the company of men, if my father is not present."

To this the hermit replied,

"Wisely said, young maiden. Now cast aside those pearls you wear about your neck for they do not befit a modest woman such as yourself."

The maiden did not want to cast aside her beloved pearl necklace for it was a gift from her grandmother but fearing that her own vanity might cause the old hermit to stumble and knowing that her grandmother would understand, she took off her necklace and cast it into a deep ravine and walked home without it.

Some weeks later, the maiden again walked in the forest and heard the hermit's voice. She listened closely and once more was convinced that he was reciting something from the book.

When the hermit noticed her this time he did not shout

but beckoned her in the most gracious voice she had ever heard.

"Kindly enter my dwelling as you are always welcome here."

She replied as before,

"I cannot, for I am a maiden and am forbidden the company of men if my father is not present."

Again the hermit replied,

"Wisely said, young maiden. Now cast aside your garments for the Creator of us all hath clothed thee well and He hath clothed the birds of the air, more than Solomon in all his glory, and such vanities as garments do not befit a modest woman such as yourself."

This frightened the maiden but she could not hold her tongue for she knew such a teaching was not to be found in all the pages of the book she loved nor any other book one might consult for wisdom. So she answered.

"Yes, the birds of the air are clothed as you say. But by garments we're covered in the very same way."

At once the hermit changed into a prince clothed in royal attire and spoke as one saved from some great disaster.

"Thanks to whomever provided you with the book of wisdom that you hold so dear for your wise and modest words have freed me from a curse that was placed upon me many years ago. As a young man, I thought I knew all things and felt quite sure that I would win when I wagered that I could find a maiden who was beautiful, modest, and wise. Should I find such a one, my gain would be the wealth of the sorcerer and the maiden as my bride. The sorcerer would surrender himself for imprisonment forever. My loss would be to remain a lonely hermit till my death. So you see, my most precious maiden, you have not only freed me from the sorcerer's curse, but you have saved the kingdom from the wicked sorcerer himself. Yes, for today, your wise and modest words have sent him to the dungeon where he belongs. May it ever be known that you have thrown aside your vanity yet have retained your virtue and may you be an example for all to follow. I would ask you to be my wife but alas, I know to accept an offer of a prince to be his princess would be a vain thing indeed and you would surely refuse me."

To which the beautiful, wise, and modest maiden replied.

"If I must choose between vanities and foolishness I shall choose vanities for a fool remains a fool no matter what the reason and such would be any maiden who would refuse the proposal of a prince such as yourself. But the king's subjects one and all shall have no difficulty forgiving the vain failings of a poor forest maiden whom the prince would honor to wed."

In an instant the Prince and his new found bride, who surely was beautiful, modest, and wise, were transported to the King's court and their garments magically transformed to those of a Prince and his Princess ready to be wed. The maiden's family was fetched in a royal carriage and the prince and his bride were married. And it goes without saying but we shall say it nonetheless: They lived happily ever after.

The moral of this story is that great rewards await those who value modesty, simple beauty, and wisdom. Are there books that you value for their wisdom? I hope so. We can all use a little extra wisdom. Our next Fairy Tale is:

Voice in the Trees

VOICE IN THE TREES

Once upon a time there was a girl whose family worked in the orchards of a wicked sorcerer. Although her family did not wish to work for the sorcerer, they had no choice for they were very poor. Their home was a shack beneath the trees and even though their life was hard, they were happy for they had each other. One day, as the girl pulled her fruit cart through the trees, she heard a voice. It was faint but she could make out the words,

"Come hither my love, come hither."

Come hither in fairy tales they use to say come here but it sounds a little different and fun, doesn't it.

Now the girl wondered who would call her 'my love' but was afraid to find out for the sun had already set. Even so, she was curious enough that she took her father's guard dog and ventured into the orchards that night. She walked deeper and deeper keeping the dog close by her side. Back and forth she wandered, looking for who it might be that had called her. Before long, she was quite lost for the sorcerer's orchards continued for miles. When she'd lost all hope of finding her way back, she sat down and cried, knowing that she would have to spend the entire night in the orchards. Then she heard another voice. It was her father's dog. Her father had told her that the dog talked but she thought he was just making up a fairy tale as he was fond of doing. Now the dog was telling her the same tale that her father had told her, only this time she was witnessing the dog talking to her face to face! The dog said,

"I was valet to the prince and was his most trusted body guard on that cursed night that the sorcerer seized the kingdom. He used black magic to banish the prince, to bewitch others, and to cast a spell that made animals of those who refused to serve him. The voice you heard is that of one loyal to the prince."

"So it is not an evil voice?" The girl asked. "But it is the voice of one I can trust?"

"Yes, you can trust him as do many others do."

"So who is the one that beckons me?" The girl asked.

"I am forbidden from telling or I should cost the prince himself his life but I assure you, the one whose voice you hear shall bring you no harm. But it is dangerous for me to speak. I shall speak no more this night."

The girl's fear of the sorcerer's orchard had vanished by now, since she realized the dog could lead her home. So she got up and started walking. As she walked, she remembered the words of her father. He would repeat them to her each night as he tucked her into bed.

"No matter where you are, I walk with you. Where you sit, I sit, and where you lay down, I lay down."

As the girl walked through the orchard she could feel the presence of her father for she knew he was with her in spirit, even by her side. So she sang this song to him;

"My father is great in the forest

He follows wherever I go

He walks with me side by side

His love for me overflows"

As she sang, she again heard the voice in the forest as it seemed to sing with her.

"Your father is great in the forest

He follows wherever you go.

And another shall soon take his place

As into a maiden you grow."

At once the girl was transported to her porch and she was startled when her father woke her with his gentle touch saying,

"Come inside, you have been dreaming here on the porch. Sing me your songs for I cannot sleep without them."

After the girl sang to her father, she told him what she now thought was but a dream; how she had followed the voice into the orchard, about the song, and how she found herself back on her own porch in an instant. But she didn't tell him that the dog had spoken to her for she feared he would think she was bewitched.

Her father listened and nodded for he was beloved to her for good reason. He was the best listener in all the kingdom and the kindest and most loving father one could hope for. Then he said to her,

"Whether the voice is real or not, his song is true for indeed another will walk by your side as into a maiden you grow."

It was time for the girl to sing to her father as she did each night. She sang as he smiled and listened. Soon he was asleep. As the girl drifted off to sleep herself, she thought she could hear the voice singing to her once more.

"Your father is great in the forest
He follows wherever you go.
And another shall soon take his place
As into a maiden you grow."

Seven days past since first she heard the voice but this time she was more certain than ever that it was real. She followed it again, making sure to take her father's dog. This time the voice beckoned her saying,

"Sing me a song
And make me a prince
For your words give me life
And your song gives me strength."

She felt she must reply so she did with words set to her own melody. This is her song.

"When the legs of my groom bring him to me
My father will ask a great price
To be the love of my life he'll ask
That my prince pay my dowry twice."

The girl had not expected a reply from the voice but she

got one nonetheless, and it was thus.

"Twice, thrice or more
 To take your hand I'll pay
 As long as you love me
 As long as you'll say
 Yes, will you tell me now?"

This so frightened the girl that she ran from the orchard as fast as she could only to find herself once again awakened by her father on her own front porch.

"You've fallen asleep again on the porch, my love. Did your prince visit you while you slept?"

Before this, the girl had not once thought that the voice in the trees might indeed be the voice of the bewitched prince but she promised herself the next time she would ask. This time it was not seven days but seven long years till she heard the voice again but just as surely as if it were seven days she knew the voice so well for those long seven years her heart had kindled a love for him; a love so deep that nothing could end it. Now the voice in the trees sang these words to her;

"Why do you wait
Why do you linger
I am your prince
Just ask me."

The maiden, yes, the maiden, for she was no longer a little girl, was so filled with excitement that she burst forth in song with the words she had been rehearsing these seven long years.

"Are you my prince
who has come to court
Are you the one
who will live in my heart.
And are you a prince indeed
Whose love my heart has freed."

At once a man clothed in royal robes and with a vest bearing a coat of arms and a crown fell with a thud from the very tree upon which the maiden was leaning. Half dazed they both sat staring at each other.

"Indeed you have freed me." The prince said, "Your true love, that is. You have freed me from the spell that the wicked sorcerer had put upon me. Like any misfortune that might befall a prince or a poor man alike. I have learned from these seven years of imprisonment in the trees. And I shall share the blessings of freedom when I take back the kingdom from the wicked sorcerer."

The girl who by now had grown into a beautiful woman saw her simple clothing changed in an instant to a white gown of fine silk. She and the prince were now magically transported to the castle, along with her father. At once the prince bowed to her father and presented him with a scroll with the words written upon it:

"May you be graced always as a father and may I have

the hand of your maiden daughter."

His proposal was as simple as that. Then the prince proclaimed,

"Not twice, not thrice, but seven times shall I pay the dowry to wed thy maiden daughter this day."

Then he took out seven bags of coins and placed them in the hands of the maiden's father and placed a pair of golden bracelets upon the maiden's wrists.

Then he turned to the maiden and said,

"That is, if you love me."

Her answer was as simple as his proposal. "I love you." She said.

"It is done," the father declared. "Go now, enjoy your nuptials, for tonight is the marriage feast!"

The courtyard was now filled with the prince's loyal advisers. The dog, who had now turned back into a man, had returned to his regular duties as bodyguard to the prince and the people from all around had gathered in preparation for the festivities.

The prince entered the castle with his new bride as the wicked sorcerer was led away to the dungeon, forever to be banished. Then the royal herald read for all to hear:

"A new law, from the prince." He declared. "All the government lands once claimed by the prince shall be divided among the families of the kingdom, never to be sold to another, although leasing of such lands shall be permitted but for no more than fourteen years, so that each generation shall be blessed with an inheritance they can call their own. This gift, the prince gives to all, from the highest to the most poor."

And it was thus that the prince fulfilled his promise of freedom for all and served his people not by treating them as subjects but as fellow heirs to the bounty that each man and woman receives in this world.

And it goes without saying, but we shall say it nonetheless; the prince, the princess bride, and all the people of the kingdom… lived happily ever after.

Our Next Story is: **The Ragged Prince**

THE RAGGED PRINCE

Once upon a time there was a *very* rich prince who lived in a castle high upon a hill. Each morning when he woke, he would look out his window to the valley below. It was full of beautiful flowers, bountiful crops and a happy people, but alas, the prince was only rich in possessions for he had no love. The more he looked at the beautiful valley below, the more his sad heart sank for outside there was beauty but inside his castle, only loneliness.

One such morning, a stranger stood outside the castle gates and shouted.

"Let me in, let me in. I must speak with the prince!"

The guards were more in the mood to give the stranger a beating than to let him have an audience with the prince but as fortune would have it, the prince just happened to be looking out his window and shouted to the guards.

"Let him in! I tell you. Let him in!"

The prince thought to have breakfast with the stranger to find out the goings on in the kingdom. Now children, you must never talk to strangers but the prince was not a child and he was protected by his guards who thoroughly searched the stranger before letting him in the gates. As they searched, they pulled back the man's hood. It was the seer, a man who many claimed could see into the future.

This was the first time he'd visited the castle so the prince welcomed him like a favorite cousin at a family reunion.

"Ah, come in, come in."The prince greeted the seer as he walked across the courtyard. "Please join me for breakfast."

The seer sat with the prince at a table next to the fountain at the center of the courtyard.

"Now, what is so urgent that I am blessed by a seer so early in the morning?" The prince asked.

"There are times, sire," the seer said, "when I wake up in the morning and feel there is something I must do. This morning was such a morning."

"And what is it that you must do this morning, my dear seer."

"Today, I have been sent with a question for the prince."

"Ah, I am fond of answering questions. Let us seek an answer for your question." The prince said in delight for princes are known for their ability to discuss any topic under the sun.

The seer paused no further but asked the prince,

"If you could have anything, sire, what would it be?"

The Prince's heart fell for he had been hoping the seer's visit might help him forget his present sadness. Nevertheless, the seer did not lack for a reply.

"I desire true love." The prince moaned in a voice so sad that if you heard it at night you would have bad dreams. "But alas," said the prince, "Love is something I cannot buy even with all my wealth."

The seer replied,

"I cannot find true love for the prince either, even if I had the powers of heaven in my hands but I can give you something almost as precious."

"What is that?" the prince asked the seer, his eyes now shining with hope that there could be some cure for his deep sadness.

"I can give you the sounds of love and the sights of love but not the touch of love for a maiden can only give that freely. It is not something that can be bought as the prince well knows."

To this the prince answered as if in song,

"Even if I can have but the sounds of love and the sights of love, I would be happy. Pray tell, how might I get this?"

"It is not an easy thing to tell how the hand of destiny works," the seer said, "in something so great as love but here is what destiny requires of you. Spend not a cent on yourself. Depend only on the generosity of others. Pay all you want for the sounds of love and the sights of love but spend nothing for the touch of love. Now, young prince, is this agreeable to you? "

The prince surely could not have understood what was about to happen when he gave the seer his reply,

"It is agreeable."

Now the moment these words came out of the prince's

mouth, he found himself in rags outside the door of a simple village hut. Yes, in rags. Few of us have ever seen such clothing but the prince now looked like the poorest man on earth. Standing outside the hut the prince could see through the window where a maiden was playing happily with her brothers and sisters then he heard her voice. She was singing a melody so enchanting that he knew he must hear it every day of his life but the moment he discovered her, the maiden's mother came from inside demanding,

"Why are you sitting outside our hut looking in our window? You, you are filthy! Such clothing!"

To which the prince replied,

"It is true that I am filthy, kind woman, but the melody your daughter sings has found a place within my heart and each step that she takes across the floor lights my eyes with wonder. I assure you; though my clothes are rags, my heart is like a great palace for there your daughter's song echoes endlessly. If I would but shut my eyes your house might be a concert hall for the melodies that flow from your daughter's lips. As an admirer at a great concert, I would gladly pay to sit here and listen but alas, you see, I am in rags and have not one penny to give for the pleasure of hearing your daughter's voice."

The maiden's mother was amazed at the prince's poetic words and besides, she pitied him, for he looked like he'd been living on the streets all his life. His clothes were tattered and his face was dirty, so she said.

"I can see you are in great difficulty and I pity you. You may sleep outside our door tonight and listen as my daughter sings, for each night she sings a love song to me and to her father, her brothers, and her sisters."

Then the maiden's mother handed a mat and blanket to the ragged prince so that he might sleep under their stairs that night.

As the maiden' mother said, the maiden sang them to sleep. It was a love song such as the prince had never heard. He felt as if lifted by invisible wings as he drifted to sleep upon the song of the maiden.

In the morning, the maiden's mother came out and bid the prince goodbye but the prince could not bear to leave. Though he knew he had nothing, still he felt inside his pocket and could not believe his good fortune when he found a small gold coin.

"Wait," said the prince, "I have a gold coin that I will give you if I can but stay here one more day and one more night. Let me listen to the songs of your daughter this one more time."

The mother quickly agreed as her family was very poor and the gold coin would buy many weeks of food. So she took it and immediately went to the market. When she returned, she gave the ragged prince a bowl of soup and some bread.

"Take this," she said, "And may the blessings you have given us return just as surely to you."

The whole day and into the evening the maiden sang her enchanting songs and what wonderment for her voice grew more beauteous with each melody.

The next day the maiden's mother went out again and told the prince,

"I cannot allow you to sleep here again. As much as I pity you and I know that you have done us much good, but, you see, the captain of our neighborhood will come to my house and ask why I am allowing a beggar to sleep under our steps. You… you must leave."

The prince was broken hearted when again he felt in his pocket and this time found two gold coins.

"Here," the prince said, "I do not know what providence has come to me during the night but I have two small gold coins; one for you and one for the captain of your neighborhood. Surely he will let me sleep here if you give this to him. Again the mother of the maiden agreed.

"You may sleep here tonight and tonight only. It is not right for a beggar to sleep under our steps, even if the captain of the neighborhood agrees."

The prince understood and he did not want to bring shame upon the maiden or her family. That night, as he sat quietly listening to the maiden's love songs, her mother brought him a beautifully prepared meal which he ate as he sat under the stairs of their house.

The prince felt no misfortune in the least at his ragged condition. In fact, as the he sat listening, he could not believe how greatly he had been blessed. The two days that he'd spent listening to the maiden's voice and watching her stroll about the house were the most glorious days of his entire life. If even these two days were all he had, he would know true love.

In the morning the maiden's mother came out again. This time she said,

"You really must leave now for it is not right that a beggar sleeps under our steps each and every night."

Again, the prince felt something heavy in his pockets to discover this time, his pockets were overflowing with gold coins.

"Here!" The prince said, quickly taking all the coins from his pockets and placing them into the hands of the maiden's mother. "I do not know what good fortune befalls me but now you can build a small room for me at the side of your house and use the rest to make your house more beautiful and still there will be some left to save for your future."

The maiden's mother was now overwhelmed with joy. She had never seen so many gold coins in one place and for the first time realized there was something very unusual about the ragged prince, so she agreed.

The whole day was so noisy from the workers building

the small room for the prince at the side of their house that the prince could barely hear the maiden's singing. He felt he would die missing her beloved voice but when the workers had finished, the maiden's mother laid out a new mat and new blanket and gave new clothes to the prince.

"Please bathe at the river's edge and change into these new clothes." The maiden's mother said.

The prince could not bear to be far from the maiden's presence so he ran as fast as he could to the river and bathed. When he got back, the maiden was singing again. He laid down on his mat in his new little room and slept. As the prince slept that night, the maiden's songs continued in his dreams.

Every morning that the prince awoke he would now check his pockets for there would be more and more gold each morning. This he would quickly give to the maiden's mother. Then one morning there were so many gold coins in his pockets and strewn about his little room that the floor broke through from the weight and the prince lay sprawled on top of them. The prince could not have been in greater shock except for the fact that the seer who had first spoken with him at his castle walked into his room at that very moment.

The seer spoke, "Sire, it is I, the seer. It has been a year that you have lived outside this small house and given everything you own to this family. It was my servant who came and placed the gold coins in your pockets each night from your treasury and none of your bills for the upkeep of your castle have been paid these many months. Your castle was sold this morning at auction and there is no more money in the treasury."

Now the maiden's mother entered the room so full of excitement that her words burst forth to the prince.

"We have bought the castle of the prince who disappeared one year ago. Keep your coins for today and come live with us. And if you will, take our maiden daughter for your wife. You have loved her these many months and except for the money from your pockets we would have nothing. Come, live with us and take the place of the lost prince in his castle. We will be your family and you shall be the lord of the estate."

Just then, the maiden walked in and looked upon the prince with such love that for a moment, he felt himself lifted from the ground! This time the maiden sang her song and took his hand. Then her father placed his hand on theirs and said,

"Go. Enjoy your nuptials and tomorrow we shall feast. She is yours now, new prince."

And indeed the prince *was* new for as he entered his castle for the first time in a year, he had the sounds of love, the sights of love, and now the touch of love, a gift that comes only from a bride. And from that day forward, the only difficulty the prince ever encountered was to tell when he was asleep or when he was awake for every day was a dream and each night he would dream of his days, holding his beloved bride as she sang. And it goes without saying, but we shall say it nonetheless: They lived happily ever after.

The moral of this story is that if we honor those things that are true, lovely, and pure, we will not walk alone. Thank you so much for enjoying these fairy tales with me.

Don Milton

This book was presented to:

____

On the _________ *day of* _____________________ *20* ___

By _____________________________________

sat under the stairs of their house.

The prince felt no misfortune in the least at his ragged condition. In fact, as the he sat listening, he could not believe how greatly he had been blessed. The two days that he'd spent listening to the maiden's voice and watching her stroll about the house were the most glorious days of his entire life. If even these two days were all he had, he would know true love.

In the morning the maiden's mother came out again. This time she said,

"You really must leave now for it is not right that a beggar sleeps under our steps each and every night."

Again, the prince felt something heavy in his pockets to discover this time, his pockets were overflowing with gold coins.

"Here!" The prince said, quickly taking all the coins from his pockets and placing them into the hands of the maiden's mother. "I do not know what good fortune befalls me but now you can build a small room for me at the side of your house and use the rest to make your house more beautiful and still there will be some left to save for your future."

The maiden's mother was now overwhelmed with joy. She had never seen so many gold coins in one place and for the first time realized there was something very unusual about the ragged prince, so she agreed.

The whole day was so noisy from the workers building

the small room for the prince at the side of their house that the prince could barely hear the maiden's singing. He felt he would die missing her beloved voice but when the workers had finished, the maiden's mother laid out a new mat and new blanket and gave new clothes to the prince.

"Please bathe at the river's edge and change into these new clothes." The maiden's mother said.

The prince could not bear to be far from the maiden's presence so he ran as fast as he could to the river and bathed. When he got back, the maiden was singing again. He laid down on his mat in his new little room and slept. As the prince slept that night, the maiden's songs continued in his dreams.

Every morning that the prince awoke he would now check his pockets for there would be more and more gold each morning. This he would quickly give to the maiden's mother. Then one morning there were so many gold coins in his pockets and strewn about his little room that the floor broke through from the weight and the prince lay sprawled on top of them. The prince could not have been in greater shock except for the fact that the seer who had first spoken with him at his castle walked into his room at that very moment.

The seer spoke, "Sire, it is I, the seer. It has been a year that you have lived outside this small house and given everything you own to this family. It was my servant who